TIME LOCKER

DONIELLE INGERSOLL

Contents

The Time-Travel
Adventure of Joshua William Murphy 1

PHASE TWO 18

Bullying Information
STOP BULLYING NOW
HOTLINE (USA) 1-800-273-8255 37

What Can Be Done?
SCHOOLS SHOULD HAVE
ZERO (0) TOLLERANCE FOR BULLYING 45

The Time-travel Adventure of Joshua William Murphy

Joshua saw them coming and heard the only too familiar words: "There he is! Let's get him." He quickly went over his options. He could dive into the girl's restroom, disappear into his locker or try the door to the janitor closet at the end of the hall, hoping that it would not be locked. He looked back one more time. They were gaining on him. He turned the corner and started down the hallway. The last time he tried to hide out in the girl's restroom had not ended so well. He had spent 20 minutes in the Principal's office. They called his mom and you can guess the rest of the story. He measured the distance in his mind. He would never make the janitor closet, so without giving it a second thought, he squeezed into his locker and closed the door. A few seconds later he heard running footsteps. The one in the lead would probably be Ricky. He would be followed by Jade and then Porky. Porky's name really was not Porky but some of the kids at Milton High called him that because he was big. Josh's deduction was right. The steps coming last were the heaviest. He listened until they grew fainter and fainter, then were gone. What do I do now, he mused to himself, half out loud? His best option would be to open the locker door and head in the opposite direction the bullies had gone. He then could sneak around the building, hide behind the giant Yew and watch until the field was clear. At that point he would have to take the extra time it took to go the long way home.

Joshua could not help that he was the shortest and skinniest student in high school. He had always been small for his age but at least in grade school and junior high there were other kids smaller than he, so he did not stand out quite so much. The three bullies had singled him out the very first day of school and had kept up the bullying any chance they could. They had locked him in his locker at least a dozen times. The last time they put him in upside down. He might have died had not Suzie seen them and opened the door before his neck gave way. Even though she had done that, it came with a price. She required him to do half a dozen homework assignments for her with promise of more if she ever had to help him out of a jam again. There was one thing that Porky loved to do more than lock him in his locker though. He and his buddies would corner the little fellow and drag him into the restroom. Porky would tip him upside down and douse his head in the toilet a bit before flushing it. Josh was late for class more than once because he had to hang out in the latrine drying his hair and cleaning up.

At last, everything was quiet. Today they had tried to grab him after the last class was out. That meant they were going to lock him in his locker about the time the doors were locked. Once earlier he had been stuffed in there after the closing bell, not to be rescued until the janitor came by an hour later. That was embarrassing to say the least. The following Friday night while the football game was going on Joshua had snuck into the hall with his neighbor's cordless and drilled out the rivets on the latch. He then put small pieces of wood where they had been to hold the unit in place. It helped too because the following week he had been locked up again. All it took to get out was a shove on the door and the sticks had broken, giving him his freedom. He was about to do it again when suddenly the fire alarm went off. What did that mean? School was out! Why was it ringing now? There was no need for a fire drill unless there really was a fire or, the few teachers left doing some things in their rooms needed to be warned. He decided to stay put for a little bit longer. His patience was rewarded. He heard a couple of doors open followed by some steps quickly heading for the exits. That would most likely be Jenkins and Smith. They turned left so Josh would head right. The fire alarm kept going for 15 minutes before fire sirens were heard. Then everything got deathly quiet. It was way too quiet. Joshua squirmed in his cramped quarters. He struggled against the toothpicks. They were tougher to break this time around than the last, in fact they would not budge at all. He stretched his hand up to the shelf above and fumbled around for a lighter. When he flicked it on, he saw that the rivets were back. How did that happen? Perhaps the maintenance man had noticed the broken latch and fixed it. That was not likely though because he could not keep up with half of what needed to be done around the school. Finally, out of frustration, he hit the backside of the latch as hard as he could. It must have caused it to jump enough for the door to pop open. This was a lucky break for the lad because it was Friday. Who knows how long he would have been stuck in there? A smell of sulfur entered his nostrils the moment he exited. That was strange! The only room at the high school that would have sulfur was the Chemistry room and that was two halls over.

Joshua noticed one other anomaly. The tile on the floor was laid out in a checkered pattern of black and white squares. That was just not right. Though tiled, the entire floor was the same color; at least it had been before he entered the locker. At the end of the hallway, he turned left and headed for the exit. He would be home late again. That would probably win him a lecture from his mom. She worried if he didn't get there on time. The air was hazy and smelled of smoke. Josh paused to look at the guardrail as he passed. It was brand new. The dent Jeff had made in it while in Drivers ED was gone. They must finally have replaced it. It had been hard for Jeffery to live that one down.

He had accidently hit the accelerator instead of the brake one day. Milton High had, had to lease a new Drivers ED car after that. As Josh arrived at the corner where he would normally turn toward his house, he stopped short. There was no road there at all. The entire block was gone! In its place he saw only a forest with trees. For the first time in his life, Joshua William Murphy was scared half to death. His breath started coming in short gasps. The reaction was so strong the entire contents of his stomach came rushing up and out. He just had time to bend over or it would have covered his clothes. While in that bent over position, a car passed him on the road. It was a brand new, 1950 Chevy.

Joshua looked around him. When it came right down to it nothing but the railing, the road and the High school were in the right place and the high school was brand new! It looked like it had been built yesterday. He stood there staring at it, wondering what was going on? Was he dreaming? Perhaps he had run low on oxygen while in the locker and passed out. He reached over with his right hand and pinched his left. He was rewarded with a sharp pain.

I would like to ask you a question now, reader. What would you do if one evening you started for home and nothing around you was the same as it had been that very morning? That was where Joshua found himself on May 31, 1951. When he headed off to school that morning it was May 30, 1991. By some happenstance beyond the realm of Physics he had been propelled backward in time exactly 40 years if one can account for 9 leap years. Oh! There had been rumors and legends floating around Milton from before it had ever been a town or city. An old Indian legend spoke of a 'cloud eater,' showing up out of nowhere some 250 years earlier. He had been a giant of such huge proportions the natives had named the tallest hill in the area after him. As the story goes, he was no less than 13' tall and had long, red hair. He terrorized the Indian camp for 1 hour before disappearing as quickly as he appeared.

While running after a small Indian girl, a gap opened in the air and he was gone. There were a few other strange stories of things appearing and disappearing that had floated around the high school also. Joshua heard a tale of a football disappearing into thin air while the home team was making a field goal. That had been twenty years ago. A couple of soccer games had been interrupted when the ball had suddenly faded out of sight, never to be seen again. One moment it was flying, through the air after being launched from a player's head, the next it was gone! Perhaps though, the strangest tale of all was of a football found on that same field one morning only ten years ago. Someone had used a permanent marker and written on it "Class of 1971." It was signed below that by the legendary Bobby Baker. He had been the only quarterback in the history of Milton to lead his school on to win the state championship that same year. Then there was the story of Mr. Fiddles. He would often appear in town under unusual circumstances. He had gone missing from his lab back in 1981. He was walking across that same football field one afternoon and just evaporated. Exactly a year and one day later someone swore they saw him appear out of thin air on the same field and disappear as quickly, only pausing to wave at a couple of lingering students.

After recovering a bit, Joshua headed

toward downtown Milton. Jake's Service Station was not on the corner of Fourth and Scofield. The Laundromat was no longer a Laundromat, but an eating joint called Mickey's. It was open so Josh decided to go in and have a look around. He was surprised to see that he could buy an ice cream cone for a nickel. He fumbled around in his jeans pocket until he found one. It was minted in 1960, but since it looked like any other nickel of that era, the guy at the counter paid him no mind when he exchanged it for a single dipped chocolate. Joshua was not dressed so differently from the people present. Thankfully blue jeans hadn't changed in forty years and he wore those tennis shoes that disappeared for 20 years or so and came back into style. No one seemed to notice the short kid with the ice cream cone as he left Mickey's and headed for the library. That was one building that looked the same as Joshua remembered from a couple of days ago when he went there to work on an essay for English. Once inside though and he knew it wasn't. On the periodical rack there were no magazines newer than June of 1951. The computer corner was gone and in its place were racks of reference books. A newspaper lying on a table caught the lad's attention. He picked it up and sat down on a nearby bench to read. It was then he really realized for the first time that he had entered his locker in 1991 and somehow come out of it in 1951.

Had he been less intelligent and perhaps a little younger he probably would have started bawling.

Time travel was not an unusual topic for Joshua. He rather enjoyed stories of people from all walks of life traveling through time as if it were a normal occurrence so when the realization finally dawned on him, at first, he was rather excited. Somehow, he had managed to travel to a time some 25 years before he was born. His grandfather and grandmother would still be alive out at the old farm. Dad would probably be there also although only a boy of 10? He counted the time out on his fingers to be certain. Perhaps that is where he should go next but what would he tell them?

"Hi. It's me, your grandson Joshua. You haven't met me yet, but you will in about 25 years or so. And by the way, that son of yours, don't ever let him sign up with the military." Joshua stayed in the library until five minutes before it closed. He would just have to camp out somewhere until he could figure out what to do about his situation. Just out of town he knew of a barn that would probably be there. When he woke up that morning it was old with holes in the roof and rotted siding but this evening it would probably look a lot newer or at least like it had a new paint job. Maybe he could get up into the hayloft or something and get some sleep providing they didn't have a big, bad dog guarding the premises?

Murphy looked up at the sky. It would be getting dark soon. As he listened to the wind whistling through the pine trees, he heard an owl hooting off in the distance. A short walk later he was met by a collie who escorted him to the backdoor of the barn. No one was out and about so he entered and made his way to the ladder. It was in the right place, but the boards were all in tack. Not one of them was missing as in the old barn. Up in the loft he settled down into the hay to ponder his situation.

That very morning, he had gone to school. It had been a normal day. The bullies were real and as active as they had been for the last several months. He had hidden himself in his locker to avoid getting shoved in there by them. That part didn't really make much sense, but it had happened. After all was quiet for a while, the fire alarm had gone off and he heard a couple of teachers exit the building. That was the point where things had changed. He knew it. Perhaps if he could get back into the building, he might have a better chance of figuring it all out and see if there was a way to go back? His thoughts were interrupted by the roof of the barn lighting up.

He quietly crawled over to the edge of the loft to see what was transpiring. A girl of about 9 or so entered the double door. She made her way over to a stall. There was a horse in there. It had a white patch on its head. The girl spoke softly as she approached.

"How are you doing this evening, Star? Is your baby going to come tonight? Let me have a look at you." She made her way into another stall beside the one occupied and looked at the tail end of the horse. Star lifted it up and the girl continued talking. "It looks like you may be a mommy soon. I will go in and tell old John that a new arrival may be here tonight. What shall we call him? With the moon looking all rosy and bright, I think we will call him 'Strawberry Moon.' It is going to be a he isn't it, Star or have you been holding out on me?" The horse snorted and the girl came back around to the front and gave her a small apple, dug out of a grimy pocket. The horse seemed to relish every bite. After rubbing the mare on the head for a few minutes, the girl departed. Somewhere in the back of his mind Joshua seemed to recognize her. It's like he had seen her in some photo album laying around the house or something. The resemblance only entered his consciousness for a moment then was gone. He crawled back to the spot where he had broken open a bale of hay and settled down to sleep. He was tired and completely drained emotionally. The next thing he remembered was a strong urge to head back to the school. His watch showed 3 am.

The night was bright. Just as the girl has said, a full moon hung over the barn as he exited. The collie came up and followed him to the edge of the property. He reached down and petted him on the head. He seemed to appreciate it.

"Keep your eyes on that girl for me, Lassie," he stated as he opened a little gate and headed back to school. "Someday she will grow up to be my mother." Back at the school a thick haze seemed to engulf the entire building. It showed greenish in the moonlight. Perhaps there really had been a fire and the building was still smoking? If he could get in there maybe, some answers would come. He entered the fog and made his way to the back, double doors. To his surprise the one on the right opened. Looking down he saw that someone, probably a student, had placed thick tape over the door catch. So, things hadn't changed much in 40 years, at least in that respect? Inside he made his way to the first hallway and turned toward his locker. When he got there, he opened it up. He was surprised to see all his stuff in it just as he had left it. The lighter was on the shelf. There was a picture of Sandy hidden behind his lab coat. She was his secret girlfriend. Not that she gave him any notice. No, not whimsy, little Joshua. The only thing different were the rivets? What to do now? Should he try and squeeze back inside and wait? It was worth a try but what if he wasn't so lucky with the latch this time? What if it didn't pop open again? He had been given a lucky break last time, perhaps it wouldn't be so this time around? He should at least try but try as he might he could not fit inside. Had the locker shrunk?

Out of frustration he grabbed the lighter and headed back down the hall. The tile squares were still black and white but outside the haze had lifted. The moon had risen higher in the sky. Without thinking he headed toward the football field. About halfway to the north goal posts a slit in the air opened. Out walked an older man in a lab coat. When he saw Joshua, he smiled and waved then disappeared into another rift. The boy was running now. He had to get some answers. The time vortex was still open. He could make it, he had to make it. He ran like he had never run before. The ground raced away under his feet. Up ahead he nearly ran into the guard rail. There was a large dent in it. Joshua reached down and kissed it. The road to his house was where it should be. As he passed Mr. Fiddles house, he noticed a light on in the lab for the first time in years.

Joshua looked at his watch. It had a calendar on it. The time was 4.30 am. The date was June 2, 1991. A complete day had been lost. Oh, it existed somewhere in a time warp. There was a time vortex somewhere close to Milton High but this morning it was no longer operating. Josh slipped in the back door, crept up the stairs avoiding each of the 3 creaky steps. School would be out in 5 days. He would finally get a rest from Porky and his thugs. As he looked in the mirror while undressing, he noticed that his pants were very tight. There was at least six inches of bare leg showing from the bottom of his jeans to the top of his shoes. His shirt sleeves were also short, and the garment felt tight around his chest. Three buttons had popped off from it.

PHASE TWO

Joshua was aroused from his slumber by his mother calling.

"Joshua, honey, are you getting up soon?" The question somehow made it through the cobwebs of his mind. He stretched and yawned before answering.

"Maybe in about half an hour or so. I didn't get a lot of sleep last night."

"Are you alright, hon? Your voice sounds like you are coming down with a cold. It is really deep." Joshua had to think about that one before sending a response down the stairs to where his mother was.

"I am fine, Mom. Just really groggy, that's all. I may sleep a bit longer. I can't seem to clear my head."

"I was going to ask you if you wanted to take a trip to the city with me. I need to do some shopping there. I am getting low on supplies and am going to WalMart. I need both food and some other things. But it sounds like I will be going alone. Is there anything you need with summer coming up?"

Josh really woke up now. He sat up in bed and pondered her question. He wondered if the past few hours had been a dream or had he really traveled back in time. He put on a higher voice as he answered.

"Yes Mom. I think I will need some pants and shirts. Didn't you tell me I would have a growth spurt coming soon and would need some larger sizes?"

"That is usually what happens, Son. At your age, guys are a little slower at growing than gals. But once they start, they make up for it. They really take off. I will see if I can find some clothes a couple of sizes larger than you have now. If there are any sales though, I might buy some in your current size. They might be selling off some spring fashions at discounted prices." Josh was thinking clearly now. He sent a response down using his higher voice again.

"Don't bother with any sales, Mom. Just go with the bigger clothes. I think I can feel myself growing."

"It's about time. I told you it would happen. You didn't believe me, but I expect you will put on at least 5 inches, maybe more this summer. When you go back to school you will hardly be recognizable. And the gals will notice too. Just you wait and see. The school might even put you on the football team. I will check in with you when I get back. Do you have any immediate plans?"

Yes, I think Mr. Fiddles is back in town. I saw a light on at his house last night. I think I will pay him a visit."

"Ok, then, be careful around him. He has always been kind of odd." The lad heard her steps as she headed for the door. Then it was closing behind her. In a few minutes, the old pickup was backing out of the driveway. The pickup was one thing she still had left from dad. There wasn't much else. In the shed outside there were some of his clothes in plastic bags along with a few pairs of shoes. There were also some tools he had managed to collect in their short time together but that was about it. Joshua thought he would scrounge around in there a bit. He needed shoes for sure and the way his feet looked he would need some big ones. He wiggled his toes as he looked with amazement at his long legs. Where had they come from? On the floor were his shredded pants and shirt. Both had busted out the seams. He did not have a belt big enough either. Perhaps Dad had one of those he could use, also. Worse case, he could bike to the Salvation Army Store and find some things there. There was one pair of shorts his cousin had left last year when he came for a visit. He was quite a bit larger than Josh and a couple of years older. He had forgotten a few items. They would come in handy now. The young man got up and opened the bottom drawer of his dresser. He squeezed into some briefs then donned the shorts. They fit perfectly. There was a large T shirt in the drawer also. It had a picture of a faded lion on it.

"I am starving, hungry," the lad mused to himself as he bounded down the stairs two at a time. He almost stumbled and fell at the bottom. He was not familiar at all with his extended growth. It would take some getting used to. He took four eggs out of a carton and scrambled them up. Soon they were sizzling along with a couple of strips of bacon in the frying pan. The smell of the food made him even more eager to get some substance into his empty belly. He poured a large glass of orange juice and sat down to eat. Outside the sun was shining brightly. There was a breeze blowing also. The old tire swing was rocking back and forth. Since Fiddles was nearly across the street, he did not take his bike. One look at it though and he knew deep down inside he would never be riding it again.

In the shed he found some shoes that were big enough for his feet, in fact they were only one size larger than his feet. They were also tennis shoes. Dad had a couple of pair of socks that fit ok also. He was set. Now he pondered how to camouflage his height. That would not be a problem for Fiddles because it had been years since he had been in town.

It would only be natural for Joshua to have grown in that length of time. There was also the sensation his bigger size would cause at school. How was that going to turn out? The only one in town who would have those kinds of answers would be the odd scientist. He had been the only one seen walking in and out of the fabled time anomalies, anomalies that were no longer fables for the young man who had experienced them first hand.

After ringing the doorbell, it was quite a while before he saw the face of the scientist peaking at him through the blinds on the door. When he saw Josh, he smiled and opened it up.

"I have been expecting you, Joshua. Come in, come in. I am sure you probably have a lot of questions." Josh was surprised at the overly friendly response of the elder man. He had never spent a lot of time with him. It was a wonder he even knew his name. First, he had been gone for nearly two years as far as the lad could remember. Second, they had exchanged a few sentences in their previous conversations. The professor led him into a computer lab off to the left of the kitchen and bid him be seated. He took a seat behind a rather large, antique desk and looked over the top of his spectacles. Josh was amazed at the place. One entire wall was covered with monitors and sensors along with a bunch of fancy electrical boxes. Three monitors were on at the time. One showed the high school with the football field. Another showed an opening in Mount of the Clouds. Joshua had never hiked up to the cave there. Several of the kids at school had. They would take spray paint up and create some rather imaginative designs or graffiti on the rocks from time to time. Josh had never done that. His mom had a saying. "Fools Names and Fools Faces are Always Found in Public Places." So, he had not gone there. The only thing he had tried was to carve his initials along with those of his dream girl on the bark of the beech tree at the side of the old shed. A third monitor showed a landmark Joshua had only heard rumored to exist. Supposedly there was a cave about five miles away. Some said it had cave paintings in it dating way back for who knows how many centuries, perhaps millennia. The professor saw him looking around and waited patiently for him to speak.

"Yes, Professor I do have questions, a lot of them. First and foremost, what just happened?" The prof rubbed his long beard for several seconds as if pondering his response.

"You went back in time, didn't you?"

"I think I did."

"Tell me about it." Joshua jumped right in. He didn't leave anything out. He started with the locker incident first.

This drew several smiles from the bearded man. He told about the ice cream cone, the library, and the barn. Then he mentioned meeting his nine-year-old mom. He even mentioned the horse being born under the strawberry moon. Then he explained how he had felt an urgency to get back to the school and about running after Mr. Fiddles through a slit in the air. The scientists smiled at the name "Mr. Fiddles." There were several nods from him as Josh laid out the details. Finally, he responded.

"I was about your age when I first experienced the time anomalies here in the Milton area. I too had a time travel experience. I did not go back in time though like you but ahead into the future. I met my future self here in this very lab. Granted, at that time I did not have all this equipment, but I had enough to send myself back to where I started from. I told my younger self to go to the cave if he/I ever wanted to know more. This I did over several years. We traveled further into the future together and secured much of the equipment you see here. We also traveled together back in time. Right now, I can go back into my logs and see your house over several years." He flipped a few switches, and another monitor came to life. Josh saw his house. He was a small boy. His dad had come home on furlough and was carrying a very small Joshua on his shoulders.

They were laughing. He watched as his dad let him down and grabbed his arms while turning round and round in circles. Several distant memories that had been stored in some forgotten corner of the lad's mind came spring into his consciousness.

"I really have missed him." Josh heard himself muttering that under his breath. The monitor skipped ahead in time and he saw himself growing up, well at least getting bigger but not that big. Then the monitor went stationery. The monitor of the high school started to change. Josh watched as a dark, green, cloud of dust came from the crevice in the mountain and swallowed up the school. He could almost smell the Sulfur in the air as he remembered the locker. The air cleared a new school stood in the place of the older one. He watched himself leave the building then he vanished from the side of the screen. The professor now spoke.

"I have been monitoring these time vortexes for years and years. I know when they will appear and when they will go. I have entered them and exited them traveling through time for decades. When I finally caught up to my real age, young Fiddles disappeared forever. This has been a very profitable venture for me. I was able to watch the stock market from this very lab and invest money at the right time. I have made millions and millions of dollars. I went into the future and purchased technology 20 years in advance of what is available now in the world. I can do unbelievable things with this stuff. If you had the choice to choose what you would like to do with your life right now, what would it be?"

"Could I go back in time and come back the same size as when I left?" The words came blurting out from Josh's mouth. He didn't have time to think his question through.

"I could manage that for you, Joshua. But is that really what you want?"

"How are my classmates going to react when they see me nearly 7" to 8" taller than I was last Friday?"

"What do you think Porky would do, Josh?"

"You know Porky? How? As for what he would do, I don't know. I have no experience in things like this. You are the expert."

"Let's consider your options. (1) You could go back as little ol Joshua. They would probably corner you and give you a flushy, only this one would not be so nice. Since you alluded capture from them on Friday, they would think they needed to make up for it. I expect it would not be a good experience."

"How could you know that Professor?"

"I will show you." The scientist punched in a few codes on a keyboard and a monitor sprang to life from inside the school. It showed Joshua opening his locker. A big hand came from behind and covered his mouth. The little kid was hauled away to the restroom where the monitor blanked out showing only the door. The three bullies came tearing out of the door faster than he had ever seen them run before but not Josh. He never showed up. "You will die, Monday, Joshua if you go to school as the little guy." Joshua began to wring his hands. "Die. That would mean They would kill him this time?" He was shaking all over as he looked at the man behind the desk. The professor offered him a bottle of water. Joshua had never seen bottled water. This was unusual. Why would anyone put water in a plastic bottle and label it? Stupid is as stupid does. The water calmed him down.

"Is that the option you want to take, Josh?"

"No! I did not think they would really go that far as to kill me. You knew this?"

"Yes, I saw it all, Joshua. So, I turned on a time modification, weather machine I have stashed up at Cloud Point and created a time vortex that sucked you in. The timing of this event was not very good. I had to run you that far back in time to have it come out as close as it did. I did not know you would grow 7" in the process. That never figured into my calculations. So, I spent half of the night running programs to see what to do next. Do you want to see another option?"

'Yes!" The word came out of his mouth with great emphasis. "I do not feel like dying come Monday."

"Do you know what Monday is?"

"Yah, It happens every year at the beginning of the last week of school. Pretty much anything goes so far as costumes or dressing up."

"We can dress you up as little/big Joshua. Only it will not be fake. You really will be a big Joshua, all of 7 inches taller. Would you like to see what happens? I decided to dress you up in your dad's military uniform. You will come as a Marine unless you are really sensitive about your dad?" The professor hesitated a moment and continued speaking the sentence very slowly.

"Your Mom has a couple of his uniforms in the closet. There will not need to be many modifications because you are nearly his size now. You can also wear a pair of his military boots. This will give you two more inches of height. You will be about nine and a half inches taller than you were last Friday. That will put you taller than all of those bullies. Watch when you see the expression on their faces. It is priceless."

"I guess that will work if I can talk Mom into it. She is kinda partial to them. Can you show what will happen?" Fiddles nodded as he punched more codes into the keyboard. The monitor went back to the front of Joshua's locker. The lad saw a tall, uniformed military guy opening the same locker as the little kid did a few minutes ago. Porky was coming with his gang. He could see the smirk on their faces. Jade was grinning from ear to ear. Ricky had a wicked look on his face and Porky was huffing as usual. They were all dressed up. Porky had on a black cape with a giant white S, on his chest. For effects he had put some Dracula teeth over his regular ones. He had even painted the tips of the teeth red to mimic the look of blood. Ricky was dressed like a zombie. He had painted dark shadows under his eyes. He had done something to his nose too. It looked like dark, almost black blood coming from it. Jade came dressed as a Hell's Angels motorcycle dude.

Porky put his hand up to his mouth to signal to his buddies to keep quiet. He would do the talking this time. In his locker Joshua had a mirror that allowed him to see down the hall. The taller Josh was watching as the three dudes headed his way.

"Looky at what we got here. Little Joshua all dressed up in his daddy's clothes." The words came bellowing out of his mouth. He rushed up just as Joshua turned. Porky stopped dead in his tracks. His face became white as a sheet. A strong, powerful hand came out of nowhere and clutched the throat of the not so big guy, now. Joshua saw himself give it a squeeze. Porky turned from white to red as Joshua shoved him across the hallway. He slammed him into a locker on the other side of the hall and big guy slithered to the ground. His Dracula teeth went flying out of his mouth and landed at Josh's feet. Josh deliberately took his boot and crushed them into the tile. They must have been made of wax for they flattened out like a pancake.

Somehow Ricky and Jade found their running legs. They dashed back in the same direction they had come from and disappeared around the corner. Joshua leaned down to Porky. He mustered up his deepest voice and it was deep, and loud.

"Don't you ever, ever touch me again, Porky! Do you understand?" The bully on the floor was no longer a big shot. He started to cry like a baby. Joshua watched as a patch of liquid appeared between his legs and trickled unto the floor. He stammered his response.

"I, I, wiiillllneevee er touououch you again. I, I, I, proommmisse Josh. Don't hurrrtt mee ee, plleese."

The picture on the monitor changed. Joshua saw Rick and Jade exiting the door at the end of the hallway. He saw himself in close pursuit. In the courtyard he caught up with the other two bullies and grabbed each by their shirt collar. He spun them around like they were on hocky skates. The look on their faces was indeed priceless just as the professor had stated. They were not laughing at a little kid now but totally horrified. With the memory of his-what would have been his death-fresh in mind, he cracked their heads together so hard they slumped to the ground. Looking down at them there he realized how pitiful these bullies really were.

"Hey, guy's I want you to listen to me and listen real good. If I ever catch you bullying anyone in this school again. Do you know what I am going to do to you?" The two half crazed figures looking at him from the ground spoke in unison.

"No boss, we don't."

"I will tell you what I am going to do to you. You will be the ones with your heads upside-down only in place of the toilet you'll each be kissing the urinal. When I flush it, I just might unravel half a roll of TP to give it a different effect. Kinda like the frosting on the cupcake if you catch my drift. Do we have a date, girls?"

"Sure do boss," stated Jade as he rubbed a rather large goose egg that had formed on his head behind his ear.

"Yah, no problem, whatever you say, Boss," replied the other. Evidently rather than Porky, these two called him Boss.

"Oh, and about that date," continued the Marine. "I want you all dressed up real pretty like you are today only with high hills and lipstick."

"High hills, Boss? Why?"

"Because I like my girls nice and tall, and we need the lipstick to make certain there is a little color on that TP. We couldn't have the TP just look plane Jane could we now, sweethearts?" Murphy twisted his lips in a snarl as he mouthed the word "sweethearts." Jade responded this time. He was still rubbing his head.

"We sure don't, do we Ricky?" The other dude responded in a little squeaky voice hoping he was not heard.

"Nope, Jade we won't disappoint the boss will we. We will have a real nice date, just the three of us. Yup, real nice indeed."

The monitor on the wall went blank. After seeing option two Josh asked a question of the professor.

"Am I really that strong, like, could I really do that now?"

I am afraid so, Josh. I expect at this

time in your life you do not fully realize your own strength."

The End

STOP
BULLYING
NOW

BULLYINGINFORMATION
HOTLINE (USA) 1-800-273-8255

Bullying is a major problem facing people of all ages. We all have a role to play in the prevention bullying. Most people have directly or indirectly, participated in, witnessed, or experienced some form of bullying especially in schools.

There is more than one type of bullying. Let's explore some options as to how bullying can be stopped before it goes too far.

The following elements are present in all bulling: malicious intent, imbalance of power, a repeating over and over of the same behavior by those who have seized power over someone. This often causes great distress in the victim along with emotional trauma that most often leads the victim to have a low esteem of themselves.

Types of Bullying

1. Direct Bullying and Indirect Bullying

Direct bullying is different from indirect bullying as direct bullying involves direct contact with the one being bullied. Indirect may not.

2. Physical Bullying

Physical bullying always involves physical contact with the other person. In most cases it is a hands-on contact, but can also include throwing items, tripping, or physically harming or forcing others to bring physical harm to a person.

3. Emotional Bullying

Emotional bullying exercises ways and means to bring emotional hurt to another person. This can include saying or writing hurtful things, causing others to gang up on an individual, purposeful ignoring, or spreading rumors.

4. Sexual Bullying

Sexual bullying refers to any sort of bullying, done in any manner, that is related to a person's gender or sexuality. Examples can include forcing someone to commit intimate acts, making sexual comments, or unwanted touching.

5. Verbal Bullying

Verbal bullying means using any form of language to cause the other person distress. Examples include using profanities, hurtful language, negatively commenting on a person's appearance, using derogatory terms, or teasing.

State Anti-Bullying Laws

All states in the U.S. have anti-bullying laws, although they can vary. These include a requirement for schools to report, document, and investigate cases of bullying at their physicality's. Schools are also required by law to take action to stop bullying. Some state laws may list consequences for bullies, and mandate that bullied students be offered proper counseling.

1. More than one out of five students report being bullied in their life

2. Bullied students reported that bullying occurred in the following places:

- 42% in the hallway or stairwell at school

- 34% inside the classroom

- 22% in the cafeteria

- 19% outside on school grounds

- 10% on the school bus

- 9% in the bathroom or locker room

3. The reasons for being bullied reported most often by students include:

- Physical appearance

- Race/ethnicity

- Gender

- Disability

- Religion

- Sexual orientation

4. School-based bullying prevention programs decrease bullying by up to 25%

Effects of Bullying: How Bullying Affects Children?

The Consequences

Those who have experienced bullying can have low self-esteem which can lead to depression. Some victims of bullying have physical and/or emotional distress as a result of school bullying. Adolescents who were bullied are more likely to develop depression in adulthood.

Chronic Victimhood

Unfortunately, some students are victims of chronic bullying, occurring multiple times a week. This is more common in elementary school.

What are the Main Causes of Bullying?

There are many factors that come into play that can result in bullying. If there are students that have tendencies towards bullying, and the school climate allows it, bullying is likely to occur. Bullying can be a result of a difficult home situation, low self-esteem, or poor social skills.

What to Do If Your Child is Bullied?

It is hard on a parent to find out their child is being bullied, but know that you can do something about it.

First, make sure to document the instance of bullying getting as many details as you can. You should also document the impact it has on your child to help the school understand how bullying is affecting the child's education. Check if the bullying has violated any laws, and finally, submit a complaint via email about the bullying to your child's school.

Reluctance to Report

A majority of students do not report bullying in schools to adults. This can be due to fear of retaliation, not wanting to worry parents, being ashamed that they can't defend themselves, feeling that nothing can change the situation, and fearing the teacher or parent would make the situation worse.

There is also a reluctance to report witnessing an incident, for similar reasons. Reporting bullying will increase with anti-bullying programs because students will feel more confident in their own abilities to intervene, and the abilities of the school to make a difference.

Victims of Bullying

Most bullies bully children in their same grade at school, but sometimes the bully is older. Having a large circle of friends tends to reduce the likelihood of a child being bullied, while a slightly physically weaker, smaller and nonassertive child has a higher likelihood of being bullied.

What Works To Prevent Bullying?

Schools need to have policies in place and procedures that are enforced. Bringing anti-bullying into every part of the curriculum can also go a long way. For example, language arts teachers can find required novels that give students empathy for others.

Why Children Become Bullies at School?

It was thought that bullies had low self-esteem and bullied to make themselves feel better, or their home environment was the greatest contribution to this problem.

Now with continued research, new evidence indicates that bullies are higher on the social ladder and push others down to remain on the top.

Bullying Behavior

Bullying occurs in every area of the world, despite vast cultural differences between some countries.

With girls, bullying is most likely to be indirect and they bully other girls.

With boys, bullying is usually direct, and boys will bully both boys and girls. Boys tend to bully more than girls do, and in many cases, bullying occurs in groups. Bullying in schools tends to decline around age 14-15.

What Makes a Bully?

School bullies tend to share common traits such as aggressive, dominant, slightly lower than average intelligence and reading ability, and are of average school popularity. Many suggest that bullies may have poor social skills, have low empathy levels, and can be uncooperative.

What Can Be Done?

SCHOOLS SHOULD HAVE ZERO TOLLERANCE FOR BULLYING

1. What is School Climate?

School climate is the overall quality and character of school life. A positive school climate goes a long way in preventing bullying in schools. Teachers and administrators can encourage a positive school climate by implementing the following:

2. Teach Kindness and Empathy

Children should know from an early age what effect their behavior has on others. They should be taught to see others' perspectives to help them understand other people emotionally.

3. Identify Gateway Behaviors and Warning Signs

Teachers are often busy, but if time is spent identifying warning signs of bullying and stopping these small behaviors right away, future distress can be avoided. Examples of 'gateway behaviors' include eye rolling, name calling, prolonged staring, back turning, ignoring, and laughing cruelly or encouraging others to laugh.

4. Create Opportunities for Connections

Make the school or classroom feel like a community. When students feel that their peers are part of their group or community, they will be less likely to bully and more likely to stand up to other students bullying and breaking apart the community they helped build.

5. Use the Arts

The arts can be a powerful tool in helping students reflect and express themselves when it comes to bullying in schools. For example, students could write a creative story about bullying. There could be a competition to create artistic anti-bullying posters that will be put up around the school, and the top 3 receive a reward. The possibilities are endless.

6. Participate in Simulations

A fun interactive idea to help reduce bullying in school is having students participate in simulations together. Have a class act out a bullying situation together and explore alternative ways to handle conflict. This will increase their empathy and help them come together to come up with bullying solutions.

7. Bring Peaceful Solutions

Peaceful solutions are the answers to bullying, not spreading more hate. Do not bully a bully, or encourage hate or violence in the student being bullied.

8. Remove Labels, Address Behaviors

Labeling a child as a bully does not help the situation. Teachers and parents should look at bullying behaviors instead of identifying who is a "bully."

9. Set Clear, Enforceable Rules

If bullying is a part of school and classroom rules, there is likely to be better prevention of bullying in schools. Rules should be in positive terms, cover multiple scenarios, and be age-appropriate.

10. Reward Positive Behavior

When students do something bad, they are called out. When a student does something good, it is important to bring attention to that as well. This shows the classroom that bad attention isn't the only type of attention.

11. Use Open Communication

Communication is key with bullying prevention. When children feel like they can talk to adults in their community, they are more likely to report bullying, and to avoid bullying by working out their feelings verbally.

12. Monitor Hot Spots

Identify areas of school, or certain sites that seem to have lots of bullying incidents and have a class monitor or school staff patrol the area.

13. Each Child is Different

Remember that every child will respond differently to being bullied, and when reprimanded for bullying. Tailor your methods to the individual child.

14. Listen!

Ask questions, stay involved, and be in the know about what is happening at school.

15. Take Actions

If you find out that there is bullying happening at school, take steps to prevent it. Start by identifying the situation and brainstorming causes. Talk to your child if you are a parent, or all children involved if you are a teacher. Come up with an action plan to prevent the bullying, and clear next steps if this doesn't stop.

16. Connect

Help your child or student connect with other friends by setting up play groups, study sessions, or offer to drive them to friends' houses on the weekends. The more connected your child is, the less likely they will be bullied.

17. Trust That Your Child Will Be Ok

It can be difficult to know that your own child is being bullied, but with your support and efforts it can go away. Remember that with time, your child will be okay.

Is There Anything I Can Do If I Observe Bullying?

Of course! Stand up for the student, and let the bully know that bullying is not okay. Interrupt the bullying safely by asking the bully a question or asking them to go somewhere with you. If you feel uncomfortable stepping in; contact an adult as soon as possible. Make sure to report the incident.

Bullying in schools is a tough issue to tackle, but if schools, parents, and students all commit to stopping prevention and action, it can be stopped.

(FOOTNOTE) "Borrowed in part from a web article by University of the People: Educational Revolution"